IT'S A GROOVY WORLD, ALFREDO!

In memory of Adrian Mitchell, 1932–2008.

He pulled music, unicorns, pirates and rockets

from his magical coat of umpteen pockets... – ST

To Mum, Dad and Paul for their encouragement,

Alison, Tamlyn and Caroline for their support,

and Rikke for her patience and understanding. – CG

First published 2015 by Walker Books Ltd, 87 Vauxhall Walk, London SE11 5HJ • 2 4 6 8 10 9 7 5 3 1 • Text © 2015 Sean Taylor • Illustrations © 2015 Chris Garbutt • The right of Sean Taylor and Chris Garbutt to be identified as author and illustrator respectively of this work has been asserted by them in accordance with the Copyright, Designs and Patents Act 1988 • This book has been typeset in Burbank Big • Printed in China •
• British Library Cataloguing in Publication Data: a catalogue record for this book is available from the British Library • ISBN 978-1-4063-2413-6 • **www.walker.co.uk**

IT'S A GROOVY WORLD, ALFREDO!

Sean Taylor illustrated by Chris Garbutt

WALKER BOOKS
AND SUBSIDIARIES
LONDON • BOSTON • SYDNEY • AUCKLAND

"Hello, Alfredo!" said Marty. "Rick's having a birthday party with disco lights and groovy dancing! And you're invited."

"I don't like groovy dancing," said Alfredo.

"You've got to like groovy dancing," replied Marty. "It's a groovy world, Alfredo!"

"But everyone laughs at me," Alfredo told him.

"Not any more, they won't," said Marty. "Because I can teach you everything you need to know."

"OK," nodded Marty, when he arrived at Alfredo's house. "There are three ways of groovy dancing in the world.

And the first one is called

COOL BOOGIE STYLE.

You bend your knees.

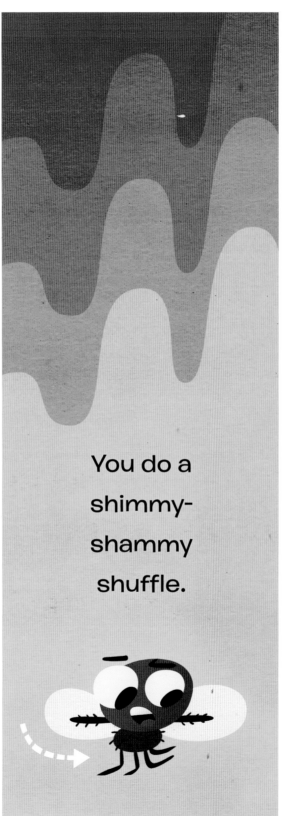

You do a shimmy-shammy shuffle.

Then you make sudden cool moves like this."

Alfredo bent
his knees.

He tried a
shimmy-shammy
shuffle.

Then he
went ...

JUMP! JUMP! JUMP!

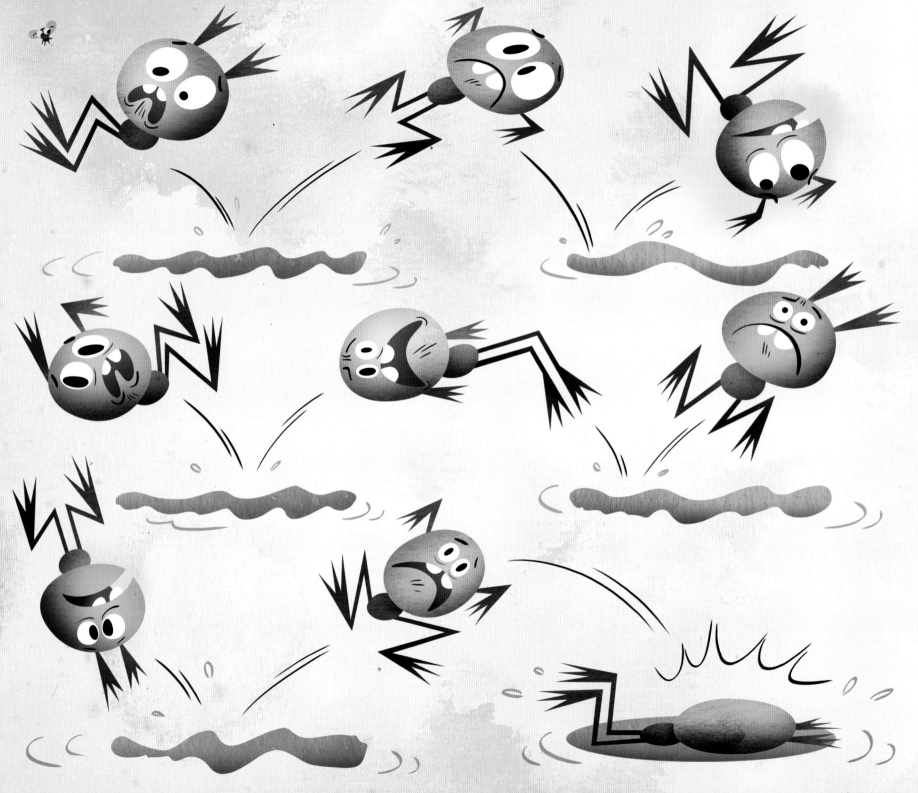

"You went JUMP JUMP JUMP," said Marty.

"That's why everyone laughs at me," said Alfredo. "It always happens."

"Next time, just let the rhythm take control," Marty told him. "Then everything will be fine."

"What's the second way of groovy dancing?" asked Alfredo.

"It's called the
SPEEDY HEEBIE-JEEBIES,"
said Marty.

Alfredo tried to let the rhythm take control.

He nodded his head.

He hopped from foot to foot.

He lifted his arms in the air. Then he went ...

JUMP! JUMP! JUMP!

"I went JUMP JUMP JUMP again," said Alfredo.

"You looked like a duck on a trampoline," Marty told him.

There was silence for a moment.

"Say to yourself: supercool dancer, yes!
Duck on a trampoline, no!"

"Let's try the next way of groovy
dancing," suggested Alfredo.

"The third way of groovy
dancing is called

SILKY-SMOOTH MOVING AND GROOVING," said Marty.

"You sway your hips.

You tap your toes.

You make smoochie-coochie hand movements.

Then you spin around. And you KEEP YOUR FEET ON THE GROUND!"

Alfredo
swayed his
hips.

He tapped
his toes.

He made
smoochie-
coochie hand
movements.

Then he
spun around
and went ...

"I wish I could dance but I definitely don't think I can," sighed Alfredo.

"Let's just go to the party," said Marty. "Once the music is playing, the rhythm will take control of you, no problem."

At the party, the rhythm took control of Marty, no problem.

He bent
his knees.

He did a
shimmy-
shammy
shuffle.

And he
made
sudden cool
moves.

"Let's
dance,
Alfredo!"
called
out Rick.

But Alfredo sat down with some others who were sitting down.
"I can't dance because I'm too hot," he said.

Marty and Rick started doing the Speedy Heebie-Jeebies.

"IT'S A GROOVY WORLD, ALFREDO!" called out Marty.

"I know. But I can't dance because I need to go to the toilet," said Alfredo.

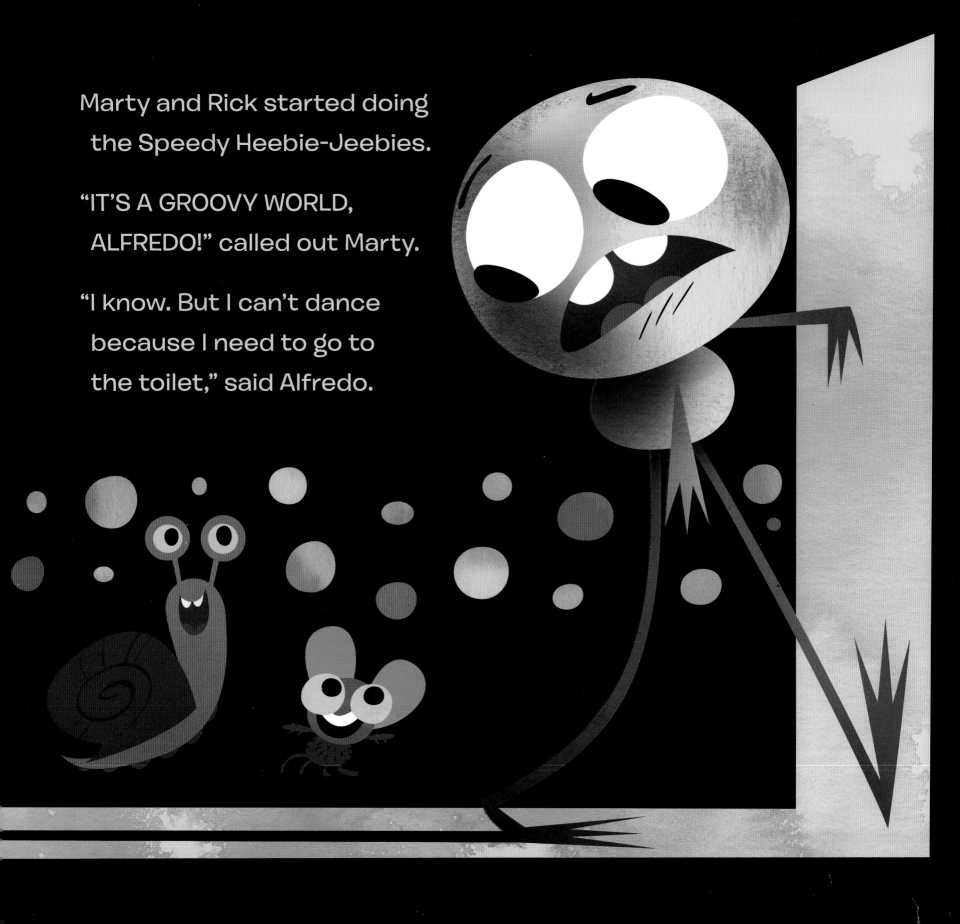

When he came back, some of the others who'd been sitting down were standing up and dancing.

The music did seem to be very groovy.

Alfredo started to tap his toes.

In fact he felt as if the rhythm might be taking control.

So he got up. He swayed his hips.

"That's it, Alfredo!" called out Marty.

He tapped his toes.

"YEAH!" said Rick.

He tried some smoochie-coochie hand movements.

"You've got it!" nodded Marty.

Alfredo checked to make sure his feet were still on the ground. Then he spun around. And he went ...

Alfredo squeezed
his eyes shut.
He knew he
was green with
embarrassment.

He knew he looked
like a duck on a
trampoline.

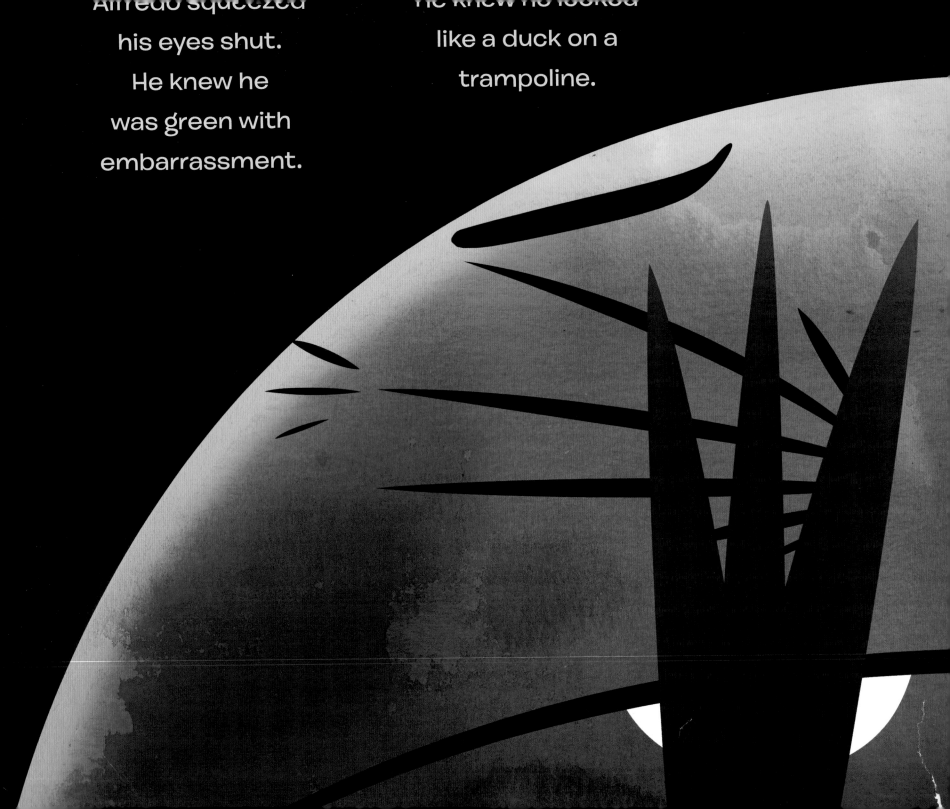

He knew everyone was going to laugh.

But he couldn't hear laughing.

What he could hear was ...

JUMP!
JUMP!
JUMP!

Some of the others were copying him. Even some of the ones who'd been sitting down.

Soon, just about everybody at the party was jumping like Alfredo. And when Marty and Rick saw what was going on, they started jumping, too.

"This is pretty good when you actually try it!" called out Marty.

"It's the fourth way of groovy dancing!" added Rick.

"I know!" said Alfredo.
"It's called the ...

JUMP-JUMP-JUMPING JIVE!"